'Tis the good reader that makes the good book.
Ralph Waldo Emerson

For
Rick

BLESS US ALL

A Child's Yearbook of Blessings

Cynthia Rylant

Simon & Schuster Books for Young Readers

JANUARY

Bless the houses
snug and tight,

Bless the kitties
day and night,

Bless the trees
and bless the snow,

Bless us all
when cold winds blow!

FEBRUARY

Bless the ones
who love each other,

Bless the grandpa
and grandmother,

Bless all pets
in wintertime,

I'll bless yours
and you bless mine.

MARCH

Bless the whoosh
that takes our hats,

Bless the dogs
and kitty cats,

Bless the crocus
and the trees,

Bless the birds
and God bless me!

APRIL

Bless the raindrops
from the sky,

Bless the babies
rolling by,

Bless all papas
with their pups,

Bless the cats
and buttercups.

MAY

Bless the buds
that bloom each spring,

Bless the birds
who come to sing,

Bless the little
sleepyheads,

And the pets
beside their beds.

JUNE

Bless the flowers,
bless the bees,

Bless the birds
above the trees,

Bless the bunnies,
kitties too,

Bless each day,
all warm and blue.

JULY

Bless the shining
stars at night,

Bless the colors
blazing bright,

Bless good friends
who watch the show,

Bless the nighttime
all aglow.

AUGUST

Bless the children
who read stories

Underneath
the morning glories,

Bless each dog
and kitty too,

Bless us all
'til summer's through.

SEPTEMBER

Bless the buses,
bless the mamas,

Bless the babies
in pajamas,

Bless the ones
who go to learn,

Dogs will wait
'til they return.

OCTOBER

Bless the mountains,
bless the oaks,

Bless the children
and their folks,

Bless the trees
in autumntime,

As they shimmer,
as they shine.

NOVEMBER

Bless the beans,
bless the bread,

Bless the puppies
being fed,

Bless all those
so dear to us,

Keep them safe
and near to us.

DECEMBER

Bless the earth
and those who love it,

Bless the angels
up above it,

Bless the wonders,
bless the glories,

Bless the world
and all its stories.

SIMON & SCHUSTER BOOKS FOR YOUNG READERS

An imprint of Simon & Schuster Children's Publishing Division

1230 Avenue of the Americas, New York, New York 10020

Book design by Anahid Hamparian and Cynthia Rylant

The text for this book is set in 25-point Colossalis.

The illustrations were rendered using acrylics and fabric.

Printed in Hong Kong

First Edition

10 9 8 7 6 5 4 3 2 1

Library of Congress Cataloging-in-Publication Data

Rylant, Cynthia.

a child's yearbook of blessings / Cynthia Rylant.—1st ed.

p.   cm.

on of twelve bedtime blessings, one for each month of the year.

ISBN 0-689-82370-3

and devotions—English. 2. Devotional calendars—Juvenile literature.

[1. Prayer books and devotions.] I. Title.

BL625.5.R95   1998

291.4'33—dc21

98-4395

Also available from Penguin—James Lipton's classic gift to word-lovers everywhere

An Exaltation of Larks

and 1,000 more group terms, real and fanciful, from the 15th to the 21st centuries

An Ostentation of Peacocks

A Skulk of Foxes

A Shrewdness of Apes

A Leap of Leopards

A Score of Bachelors

An Unction of Undertakers

A Click of Photographers

A Wince of Dentists

A Lot of Realtors

If you've ever wondered whether familiar terms like "a pride of lions" or "a string of ponies" were only the tip of a linguistic iceberg, James Lipton's charming collection of collective nouns provides the definitive answer. Infectious in spirit and beautifully illustrated with more than 250 witty engravings, *An Exaltation of Larks* is a word lover's garden of delights.

"James Lipton has performed all speakers of English a great service. If there were an English Academy, he would surely deserve election."

—Raymond Sokolov, *Newsweek*

ISBN 978-0-14-017096-2